Scales began to blow hotter and hotter gusts of air into the balloon and the balloon began to grow bigger and bigger until it was struggling to get off the ground.

"Quick! Now, jump in!'

They jumped, they scrambled, they were in and – they were off!

What a lovely, thrilling, fearful thing flight was! Bright with beauty and sharp with danger. Sam laughed and stared and glowed and gasped.

Then Scales stopped breathing hot air up into the balloon and let it sink lower and lower till – bump, it hit the ground! The balloon sagged sideways, the basket tipped over, and the three of them spilled out!

'Oh, oh,' laughed Sam and Christopher, untangling themselves, 'that was fun!'

'It was,' Scales agreed, 'but it's not for fun I've brought you here. Magic Mountain is in danger and needs your help!

Dragon in Top Class is the fourth title in a lively and amusing series about Sam and his special dragon friend, Scales.

Also available by June Counsel,
and published by Yearling Books:

A DRAGON IN CLASS 4
A DRAGON IN SPRING-TERM
A DRAGON IN SUMMER

JUNE COUNSEL
DRAGON IN TOP CLASS

Illustrated by James Mayhew

CORGI YEARLING BOOKS

DRAGON IN TOP CLASS
A YEARLING BOOK 0 440 86321 X

First published in Great Britain by Doubleday,
a division of Transworld Publishers Ltd

PRINTING HISTORY
Doubleday edition published 1994
Yearling edition published 1995

Text copyright © 1994 by June Counsel
Illustrations copyright © 1994 by James Mayhew

Set in Linotron Bembo by Chippendale Type Ltd

Yearling Books are published by Transworld Publishers Ltd,
61–63 Uxbridge Road, Ealing, London W5 5SA, in
Australia by Transworld Publishers (Australia) Pty Ltd,
15–25 Helles Avenue, Moorebank, NSW 2170, and in
New Zealand by Transworld Publishers (NZ) Ltd,
3 William Pickering Drive, Albany, Auckland.

Printed and bound in Great Britain by
Cox & Wyman Ltd, Reading, Berkshire

Again, for Alan

CONTENTS

1 Wings

Flying along the lane to school this sparkling September morning, Sam stopped at the Rec to look across at the baby swings because it was in one of those baby swings that he'd first seen Scales, the baby dragon, who was now his friend! A year ago today, thought Sam, and now I'm Top Class and Scales will be Top Class, too.

He walked into the Rec and stood looking round. There were new baby swings, but not brightly coloured like the old ones. These had bars and seats of solid rubber, black or dull orange. Under the big swings, instead of concrete, were squares of the same solid rubber. The roundabout had gone and there was a new slide, much lower and tamer than the old one. There was now a seat for parents and a litter-bin. It was tidy and safe, but not exciting, and Sam was glad he'd known the Rec when the slide was high and there was a roundabout that could be whirled faster and faster and faster, because what one wants, thought Sam, is excitement.

He swished at the grass. Shining, winged things, seeds and insects, flew up and flickered away. He saw a feather quivering on a grass stem and picked it off; such a shining, shimmering morning as though the air were dancing.

'Oh, Scales,' he called, 'you would *love* it!' And – there *was* Scales with butterflies zigzagging between his spines and tiny beetles in jewelled wingcases running over his claws.

'I heard you call, Sam, and I thought, oh good, term's started. Hang on to my front claws and I'll hang-glide you to school.'

He rose up, and Sam put up his hands and caught hold of the strong curved claws and – wow! – they were off! A glorious way to go to school, even though the air rushed past like iced water and he could hardly breathe.

Bump! Scales dropped him gently on to

the Infant grass by the may tree and flew off.

The bell rang and Sam raced in and up the corridor to Class 1. Class 1 was like a barn, a big old classroom that had been the *whole* school when the school was first built. It had a high red wooden ceiling and brick walls. The two long walls were painted white. At one end was a raised wooden platform with a red-painted wall behind it and tall old windows. At the other end, the wall was painted green and had a green curtain right across its bottom half. Red and green, thought Sam excitedly. *Dragon* colours.

Coming in at the door, he twitched the curtain aside and gasped. Shelves and shelves and shelves piled with books, papers, boxes – all the things Mrs Green would want this term, and all the things that other teachers had wanted in other terms. It was green and dim and shadowy behind the curtain and Sam felt his spine tingle.

He dropped the curtain and walked up to the new Nature and Science Table and put his feather on it. Mrs Green nodded approvingly. 'Because,' she said, 'this term we're doing Flight!'

'*Science*,' corrected Christopher, who was clever. 'We've got the National Curriculum at home and I've done some of the experiments already.'

'Then we shall take flight on the wings of your knowledge,' Mrs Green said airily. 'Now, gather round everybody, and listen to your names and tables. Sam, you're on GLIDERS. That's the table over by the green curtain.'

The curtain rippled gently, Mrs Green noticed. 'This is a draughty old classroom. We shall have a job keeping warm.'

Sam noticed, and felt warm with joy. *Scales* is there. He's blowing the curtain.

'Mrs Green, can Scales be in this term? He knows all about Flight.'

'If he's good,' said Mrs Green, who had never seen Scales but knew that Sam loved him. 'If he's helpful.'

The curtain rippled again. 'He will be,' said Sam. 'He's promised.'

There was a commotion at the door. A mother pushed it open and dragged in a kicking, hitting, red-haired boy. Mrs Green hurried over to her. 'Just go quickly,' she said to the mother. 'I'll take him.'

She closed the door and said cheerfully, 'Now, Russ, come and meet Ivy and Sebastian.'

The red-haired boy flung himself flat on the floor. Mrs Green pulled him up and half-pushed, half-walked him to the ROCKETS table. 'This is your chair, Russ.' But the minute she let him go, Russ slid under the table. Ivy reached her hand under to haul him back and screeched, 'Ow! He's bitten me.'

A knock came at the door. Miss Barley the Headteacher put her head round. 'Mrs Green, a minute please.' Mrs Green said, 'Class 1, help Russ while I go to

Miss Barley.' And went quickly out.

'You wicked boy!' stamped Ivy, sucking her hand. Russ put out a thumb and finger curved like a crab's claw and pinched her. Then he rushed for the door, but big Billy Bottom threw himself against it and stopped him. Sam started forward. 'Russ, come and sit with us,' but Russ jabbed him in the chest and began trying to tear Billy from the door. A claw came out from behind the green curtain and hooked Russ round the edge of it, quick as a wink.

There was complete silence. Ivy stopped sucking, Billy stopped panting, everyone – so it seemed – stopped breathing.

Then, they heard a crunching, grinding noise and a huge swallow. Class 1 went white.

'Scales,' shrieked Sam, 'you mustn't eat him!'

Scales' voice said, 'I'm just showing him what dragons *can* do.' Then the curtain whipped up and Russ shot out. He walked jerkily to the ROCKETS table and sat down. No-one spoke. Then Sebastian, who sat opposite him, said, 'His eyes are very bright! He – he's smiling!'

Mrs Green came back. 'Oh, good children, what a lovely quiet classroom. Russ, your mummy's very worried, she wants to take you home—'

'NO,' roared Russ, clenching his fist. 'I WANT TO STAY HERE!'

'Well,' said amazed Mrs Green, 'we want you to stay! So that's good.'

'It was Scales,' Class 1 told her. 'He helped.'

'Oh, did he?' said Mrs Green. 'Well, in that case . . . he can stay, but he'll find it very different from Class 4. In Top Class we're going to work very hard and learn a lot of difficult things, and he *won't* have his cave!'

'He doesn't need it. He's living behind the green curtain,' Top Class said patiently, and pointed. The green curtain billowed gently.

'That's Scales blowing,' Russ said.

'That's the draught under the door blowing,' said Mrs Green. 'Now, let us turn our minds away from Scales.' A chuckle sounded behind the green curtain. Mrs Green looked round sharply, but the curtain (and Top Class) was still and straight. 'You've all got a piece of paper in front of you. Fold it in four, now open it. You've got four squares. I want you to draw the four seasons, one in each square, because I want to find out whether you understand what we mean by seasons.'

Top Class began to draw, but Russ put his red head down on the table and burst into tears. Mrs Green rushed over to him.

'I can't *do* all this learning,' wailed Russ. 'It's too much.'

'Oh, but you can, we've got a whole *year* to do all this learning.' Mrs Green put her arm round him. 'We don't have to do it all at once. Little by little. You've no idea how clever we shall all be in a year's time!'

But when the pictures were finished, many were not all that clever. True, Billy Bottom had written *It is Spring, It is Summer, It is Autumn, It is Winter* at the bottom of his pictures, but his tree, in full leaf, stayed the same in all of them.

'It's no good drawing a caravan for Summer, Ivy. People go off in their caravans in all seasons, even winter,' Mrs Green pointed out. 'And talking of winter, Weefy, why have you put a picnic in Winter?'

'That's when we have them,' answered Weefy, who came from an odd family. 'There's too many flies in summer.'

'Well, try again, Class. Have a *think*.

Think what *trees* do, while I get on with
my display.'

She climbed up on to the platform and
began arranging books, pictures,
photographs and objects under a notice
that said: THINGS THAT TRAVEL BY
AIR. Scales came tiptoeing out through
the curtain and went up to the blackboard.
He picked up the coloured chalks and
began to draw soundlessly. The chalk

didn't even squeak. It was like magic! Top Class watched, breathless with delight but, like the chalk, not even squeaking!

'Good children,' praised Mrs Green, working away with her back to them. 'What a quiet, hardworking class. Well done. Particularly you, Russ.'

Scales finished his drawing, signed his name with a flourish, bowed to the children who raised their hands and clapped – soundlessly – and went smirking back behind the curtain.

Mrs Green turned round. 'My goodness! Who did that?' She came quickly off the platform and walked up to the blackboard, for on the blackboard Scales had drawn in vivid colours and scratchy lines: Magic Mountain in Winter, snow-covered with the dragons asleep inside; Magic Mountain in Spring, the snow melting, flowers pushing through and the dragons coming out of their cave, yawning and stretching and smiling with pleasure; Magic Mountain in Summer, the sun blazing down and the dragons basking on the rocks with the forest below green and hazy in the heat; and Magic Mountain in Autumn with a great wind blowing and the dragons lighting bonfires of leaves with their fiery breath.

'Scales did it,' shouted Top Class, laughing and clapping. Russ seized another bit of paper and began drawing furiously. 'I'm going to copy it. I'm learning!'

'I see Scales *signed* it,' said Mrs Green. 'I shan't ask who *did* it,' – at the green end of the room the curtain blew out vigorously – 'but I will accept the nom-de-plume. That's French for pen name. Another word you might like to learn is pseudonym. That's when people write or draw under a name that isn't theirs.' She wrote *nom-de-plume* and *pseudonym* on the board, but not on the picture.

'Can he stay?' asked Top Class earnestly. 'Please, can Scales stay in Top Class?'

'Looking at that picture, yes,' said Mrs Green. 'It's clear, it teaches, it's funny, it's memorable. Scales can stay!'

Top Class cheered. The bell rang. Mrs Green laughed and took her handbag off to the staffroom and Scales came out into Top Classroom, swelling and shining and smiling with conceit.

'Top Class Dragon! TCD, that's me!'

2 Bubbles

'Well, now,' said Mrs Green, 'gather round, Class, and tell me what's in this jar?'

She and Class 1 were sitting on the platform on the magic mat that Mrs Green had brought with her from Class 4.

'Nothing,' cried everyone except Christopher, 'it's empty.' But, 'Air,' said Christopher.

'Chris is right,' smiled Mrs Green. 'It looks empty, but it's not! It's full of air.

23

Put up your hands, everybody. What can you feel?'

Class 1 put their hands up. Russ waved his so hard he hit Ivy on one side and skinny Dinny Delmont on the other. Slap! Ivy hit him back. Smack! Russ hit *her* back! The green curtain at the other end of the room bulged suddenly. Russ gasped, folded his arms, sat like a stone. The green curtain flattened and hung still.

'I can feel my hair move,' cried tiny Tina. 'I'm making a wind!'

'Yes,' said Mrs Green, 'you can't *see* air, but it's there and you can use it to make things move.'

She got off the platform and walked down the classroom towards the green curtain. Class 1 held its breath. When she got to it she put her hands up, twitched it apart and put her head in. (Oh, thought Sam, it's *two* curtains, not one.) At the door end of the curtain, Scales put his head out! Mrs Green went further in. Scales came further out. He winked at Class 1

and flew up to one of the rafters and stretched himself along it. Class 1 waved to him.

'Stop fanning yourselves now, and come and sit at your tables,' Mrs Green called, coming out of the curtains with her arms full of things.

Jennie the helper came in and went swiftly round the tables with Mrs Green, taking things out of the boxes and putting them on the tables.

'Now then, we're going to do things with air! People with balloons on their tables, see if you can lift a book with your balloon. People blowing bubbles, see if you can blow a square bubble. People with straws and scissors and glue, make a windmill. Jennie will help you.'

Sam, who loved making things, particularly things that worked and were useful, made a windmill and invented a way of cutting out all the sails at once. I'm getting cleverer, he thought, and was surprised, and pleased.

Sebastian blew soap bubbles through all the different bubble spoons – square ones, oval ones, triangular ones – but *all* the bubbles came out round. Russ put his reading book on top of his balloon and blew and blew till the balloon filled and – lifted the book up!

'Science is fun, and pretty, and clever,' laughed Nargis, making a bubble picture like a field of summer flowers. 'Scales would love it.'

'Science is facts, Nargis,' Mrs Green reminded her. 'Scales is story and way above my head.'

Above her head, Scales blew at the lights

and Top Class laughed. The lights hanging from the rafters on their long chains swayed, and on the tables straws and paper rippled and lifted.

'Oh, this draughty classroom,' cried Jennie, chasing paper.

'It isn't a draught,' snapped Sebastian who was always tiresome and never more so than when he was cross and tired. 'Look up there, it's—'

But Mrs Green looked down at her watch and cried, 'Gracious, the bell will be going! Clear away, everybody.' So nobody looked up, but Scales looked down at Sebastian very hard.

When only Sam and Sebastian were left in the classroom, Scales flew down and picked up the triangular bubble spoon.

'Leave them alone,' shouted Sebastian, who was tidying. 'I'm putting them away.'

But Scales put the spoon to his lips and blew two triangular bubbles. Then he swapped the triangular spoon for a round

one ('Leave them *alone*,' shrieked
Sebastian) and blew a round bubble. The
three bubbles floated together and made
a—

'Bow tie!' cried Sam. 'You're blowing a
Sebastian, Scales!'

Sebastian clutched his bow tie and
stared. Scales blew a big round bubble that
settled on top of the bow tie bubbles, then
he blew two bubble ears, two bubble eyes

and a bubble mouth. Lastly he took the oval spoon (Sebastian too dumbfounded to say a word) and blew a long *oval* bubble and four long *thin* bubbles and there was a bubble boy, complete with body, arms and legs.

The bubble boy wavered about, looking like a transparent Sebastian, only surprised instead of furious.

'Sebastian Bubblehead,' said Scales. 'Bubblehead and bubble*mouth*.'

'Go away,' shouted Sebastian furiously, 'you can't *be* in this term. We're doing *Science*, we're doing *Air*.'

'Air,' said Scales, 'is all you've *got* in your head.' And he seized Sebastian under the arms and took him for a hang-glide round the ceiling, diving in and out of the rafters and swerving between the lights, but Sebastian didn't enjoy it.

'Put him down, Scales, please,' called Sam. 'He'll be sick.'

'I'm giving him air,' cried Scales. 'He was getting hot and red.'

He glided down and dropped Sebastian in the bin. The bin fell over and Sebastian scrambled out, arms flailing. The bubble-Sebastian floated over to help, but Sebastian's flailing arms burst it and it spattered drops all over him.

'Now you've made me wet!' yelled Sebastian.

The door began to open. Scales shot up. Jennie walked in.

'Out you go, you two, or you'll miss play. I'll finish. Oh, what a mess.'

Sam and Sebastian slipped out. Jennie set the bin up and put the rubbish back. She counted the bubble spoons. 'One missing, the square one.' She squatted down and looked under the tables. There was a tiny thud behind her. She swivelled round, saw the spoon lying near her and picked it up. Then she stood up – and gasped.

Hanging above the platform was a square bubble.

Jennie walked towards it, unbelieving.

The bubble turned itself over and over to show its six sides. It was soapy, transparent, and square. Square, no doubt about it. It floated up and up – and burst!

'I don't *believe* it,' Jennie cried.

And she didn't, though she'd seen it.

3 Hot Air!

So that was a jolly beginning to the new
term. It didn't even feel like learning. Airy
things are very uplifting, Sam thought,
they make you feel lighthearted, buoyant.
Buoyant was a word Christopher had
brought back. It means, he told Top Class,
floating.

'Wednesday afternoons,' Mrs Green had
said, 'shall be our Science Experiment
time.' So on Wednesday afternoon she
gathered Top Class round her on the
platform and told them about Air, how

strong it was, how nothing could live without it, and then they made things that used air. The very words Science and Wednesday Afternoon took on a shimmering, floating, taking-off feeling which was exciting.

This Wednesday afternoon, Top Class were making hot-air balloons; blowing up real balloons, then sticking paper over them, painting them bright colours and hanging little baskets underneath by pretend ropes of thick wool.

'It's a hazardous way of travelling,' remarked Mrs Green. 'You can make the balloon go up and you can make it come down, but you can't steer it!'

When the balloons were finished, Mrs Green and Jennie got the steps and hung the balloons on a long string across the window. The balloons with their little baskets swayed and turned in the hot air coming up from the radiator.

'Hot air currents are called thermals,' Christopher informed everyone.

'We'll put yours up later, Sam, when you've finished,' said Mrs Green, as she climbed down. 'Now, out to play, everyone.'

The classroom emptied, except for Christopher who came over to Sam and said, 'Oh, Sam, Scales will love that!'

Sam had painted a green dragon on his balloon with the four claws coming down to meet the wool ropes as though holding them.

The green curtain billowed and Scales came out.

'A Scales balloon! Let's go up in it!'

'Not possible,' said Christopher. 'It's too titchy and it needs hot air.'

Scales looked at him scornfully. 'You may be brainy, but you've *no* imagination. Hold on to me and shut your eyes.'

They did – and felt fresh cold air blowing on their cheeks!

They were on the Senior grass, miles away from even the Junior grass. 'Ooh!' gasped Sam. 'We shouldn't be here!'

'We shan't be in a minute,' Scales cheerfully assured him. 'Put the balloon on the grass with the basket towards me.'

He stretched himself along the grass with his mouth nearly touching the little basket. Very gently he blew, and the basket became a real basket and the balloon a real balloon made of strong nylon with an open mouth. Then Scales began to blow hotter and hotter gusts of air into the balloon and the balloon began to grow bigger and bigger until it was struggling to get off the ground.

'Quick! Now, jump in!'

They jumped, they scrambled, they were in and – they were off!

What a lovely, thrilling, fearful thing flight was! Bright with beauty and sharp with danger. Sam laughed and stared and glowed and gasped.

Then Scales stopped breathing hot air up into the balloon and let it sink lower and lower till – bump, it hit the ground! The balloon sagged sideways, the basket tipped

over, and the three of them spilled out!

'Oh, oh,' laughed Sam and Christopher, untangling themselves, 'that was fun!'

'It was,' Scales agreed, 'but it's not for fun I've brought you here. Magic Mountain is in danger and needs your help!'

'Is it the Frighteners?' asked Sam, remembering those terrible creatures they had met on Magic Mountain in the spring.

'Worse,' answered Scales. 'They're easily dealt with. It's the King.'

He led them down the mountain until they were slipping and sliding on shale and broken rock at the bottom. 'In here.' They ducked under a ledge and followed him into a large cave stuffed with astonishing things and full of strong smells, bubbling noises and swirls of coloured smoke.

'Magician,' called Scales. 'I've brought Sam and Christopher. They were Class 4, they're now Top Class. Christopher is brainy, Sam is brave.'

A young man in a tall pointed hat peered

at them. 'Why are all bubbles round?' he snapped at Christopher.

'Surface tension,' replied Christopher promptly, and explained.

'You needn't go on,' interrupted the Magician. '*I* know. I was just testing you. You,' he barked at Sam, 'hand me that snake.'

Through the smoky fumes, Sam saw a large snake coiled amongst the bottles and basins. Without giving himself time to think, he gripped it firmly behind the head and pulled. The snake lashed its muscular body round his arm and *squeezed*, but Sam held on. 'Here it is, Sir!' The Magician took the snake, which immediately unwound itself, and looped it round his own neck, where it lay, glistening smugly and looking at Sam.

'Well *done*, Sam,' glowed Scales, 'that *was* brave.'

The Magician nodded. 'Brave indeed.' He poured the boys a drink.

'What is it?' Christopher asked, peering at his.

'Whatever you like. Think of what you like best to drink and the drink will be that!'

Ginger wine, thought Christopher. Fizzy orange, thought Sam. They drank. 'Golly!' they gasped.

The Magician smiled sadly. 'That's easy magic. What the King wants is impossible. Listen.' And he told them the story.

'Turn Magic Mountain into *gold*!' exclaimed Sam. 'All of it? Why?'

'To astonish his neighbours *and* to keep himself rich for ever!'

'And if you can't do it?'

'He'll come with his army, kill everyone on Magic Mountain and scatter it with salt so that nothing can grow.'

'What about your dad, Scales? Can't he do anything?'

'He's away, Sam. He's taken my mum on a round–the–world flight as a two–hundredth birthday present and Aunt Spiny's gone with them.'

Sam was silent. He could not think of anything to say, except that he wanted to help. So he said that.

'There's four of us,' Christopher said. 'That's better than two. There's my brain and your magic.' He looked at the Magician. 'Scales can fly and blow hot air, and Sam – Sam is a tremendous backer-upper.'

The Magician smiled, still sadly. Scales said suddenly, 'Show us the time, Mage.' The Magician pulled a little handglass from his pocket and held it towards them. In it the boys saw a tiny picture of Top Class lining up in the playground.

Scales sprang up. 'Time we were gone! Bye, Mage, see you! Sam, Chris, *move*!'

Out of the cave; scramble, scramble up the mountain, blow, blow, blow into the balloon (hot blasts of air like the Sirocco, which is a warm wind from Africa!). Into the basket, up, up, up, Magic Mountain vanishing beneath them. Then the Senior grass coming up. Bump, out of the basket, the balloon shrinking and changing. Race to the Junior grass, scoot across the playground, tag on to the end of Top Class, *just* as it went chattering in.

'Sam,' called Mrs Green, 'you shouldn't have taken your balloon out to play! Look at its poor little basket, all bent!'

4 *Russ Stirs It Up*

'Destroy Magic Mountain!'

'Kill everyone in it?'

'Cover it with *salt*? What for?'

'To destroy plant life,' said Christopher.
'The Romans used to do it to punish tribes
who rebelled against them.'

'Oh, the Romans!' Top Class was vague
about the Romans, but very clear about
Magic Mountain. 'We've *got* to help.'

'But how?'

Top Class thought. Then, 'Help the
Magician to discover the formula to turn

the mountain into gold. It's only doing scientific experiments. You just go on till you get it right,' stated Christopher, who always got it right.

'Or ask the King to change his mind,' suggested Nargis gently.

'*Make* him change his mind,' stamped bossy Ivy Grubb, tossing her ringlets. She could make an elephant change its mind, thought Sam, she's 'bout as big as one.

'Weef, what do you think?' he asked.

Weefy Buffalo, who'd been thinking of something quite different, looked startled. 'Help the Magician in his experiments or ask the King to change his mind,' Sam explained.

'Change his mind to what?'

'Well, to not doing it.'

'He won't do that,' said Weefy. 'That's no fun. He'll want to change his mind to something better than that.'

'Let's *go*,' cried Russ, leaping up. 'Let's find *out*.'

He dashed down the classroom and

dived between the green curtains. Top Class heard his voice cry out and fade away and raced after him. The green curtain billowed out and covered them. A green dimness engulfed them, a dark darkness drew them down. A grey glimmer began, then lights and smokes and smells surrounded them, and they were *in* the Magician's cave.

'We've come to help,' announced Christopher importantly. 'So, tell us what to do.'

'I've started,' shrieked Russ, uncorking bottles, tipping their contents into a basin, seizing a spoon and stirring.

Scales took Sam to one side. 'Bad news, Sam, the King has got the witch working for him.'

'Oh!' Sam felt himself go gloomy, then he brightened. 'She tried to wreck our outing last summer, but she didn't succeed. She's not invincible.' He was proud of that word, he had found it himself. The Magician sighed; plainly he did not feel invincible. If scientists are that gloomy, thought Sam, I'm glad I'm not clever enough to be one. The Magician put his hand on Sam's shoulder and led him to a small cave where a little girl with a blank face sat staring before her.

'My daughter,' he murmured. 'The witch put a spell on her. She will not speak, nor smile, nor laugh till someone gives her a Gift of Air.'

'Of air? We're *doing* Air this term! We'll

make a Gift of Air for her, Sir, don't you worry!'

The Magician shook his head. 'I've made zephyrs and smokes and scents to please her, but nothing has worked.'

A shout from Russ brought them hurrying back to the big cave. 'I've made something! I've made something! Look, it's alive!'

He was holding out a basin of a most lively mixture, bright green with bubbles leaping up and down. 'Quick, come and watch!' He ran out of the cave followed by Top Class and flung the contents on the ground. At once every stone, pebble and boulder that the mixture splashed, turned into a frog and began hopping, leaping, croaking – the noise was deafening and the sight astonishing. Top Class fell about and the Magician shouted, 'Foolish boy, that's Frogturning Mixture. The easiest formula to mix – and the most useless.'

'I don't care,' shrieked Russ. 'I like frogs!' And he and Weefy and Billy

Bottom and Dinny Delmont (she of the red pigtails) began grabbing up the smaller frogs and putting them in their pockets – or trying to. The frogs, so lately stone, were surprisingly nimble. The boys dived and missed, slipped and tripped, clutched and caught. 'Oh, oh, oh,' laughed the girls, skipping out of the way of frogs and boys. Their voices bounced off the rocks that were not frogs, and doubled the din.

The Magician put his hands to his ears in agony.

'All right, Mage,' spluttered Scales, rolling about with laughter, 'don't despair. Russ *was* trying to help. If two minds are better than one, twenty-*two* minds must be better still!'

'Not proven,' groaned the Magician. 'Absolutely *not* proven.'

'Please, Sir,' said Sam, suddenly remembering something, 'what is a zephyr?'

The Magician took his hands down and

brightened. 'Sam! Good idea. Well thought, boy.'

He began to move his hands in gentle, flowing movements and to purse his lips and whistle softly. Nothing happened. The frog chase went rollicking on. Then, a little, soft, warm, west wind began to lift Top Class's hair and fan its hot cheeks. Nargis stood still and lifted her face. 'O-o-h, how lovely!' The shouts, screams, grabs, bounds ceased. Top Class stood, dreamy, relaxed, floating, as the gentlest of breezes, most loved of winds (the zephyr, in fact), lifted them off Magic Mountain and wafted them away and away to set them down, lightly as a feather, *in* Top Class.

Russ opened his eyes, dived his hand into his pocket, and stood dumb with joy, staring at his open palm and the frog sitting there, like a stone.

Mrs Green came in, her arms full of papers. 'Oh, children, you have been good. I'm sorry to have kept you waiting. Russ, is that a frog?'

'Yes,' said Russ, joyfully. 'I made him, out of stone.'

'Well, it's lifelike! Now, sit down everyone and – Weefy! *You've* got a frog! A giant! Is it a garden ornament?'

'I grabbed the biggest,' explained Weefy, clasping his frog to his chest.

'You certainly did! But it's too big for the classroom. Put it in the cloakroom.'

Weefy went out and into the little cloakroom used by the Baby Class and put his frog in one of the basins. 'Don't be frightened,' he said to it. 'You're stone *now* because Mrs Green wouldn't believe any frog could be this big, but you'll be real again on Magic Mountain.'

He splashed water over the frog, so that its colours shone wetly – vivid green, glistening black, gleaming yellow. Then he went back to the classroom.

'First of all,' Mrs Green was saying when he got back, 'we'll start an experiment.' She took a clean, empty milk bottle and stretched the mouth of a balloon over it. 'Now, we'll put it in a warm place on top of the radiator and see what happens.'

'The air in the bottle will get warm,' said clever Top Class, 'and expand, and blow up the balloon.'

'And the balloon will take the bottle for a ride!' cried Russ.

'Probably – not,' said Mrs Green, 'but, it might be the first flying milk bottle in history. We shall record its progress.' And she put a notebook and pencil beside the bottle.

At playtime, Sam told the others about the Magician's little daughter and the spell the witch had put on her. 'So, let's make her something splendid because if we can break the spell, the King will know that Magic Mountain's got powerful friends and he'd better keep off!'

It was Wednesday. After dinner, Top Class bounced in full of will and vigour, and curiosity. 'Let's see if the bottle's blown the balloon up yet. It's warm enough.'

It was warm. The radiator was on, the sun was streaming in, but the balloon was still hanging limply over the side of the bottle, taking no notice of science.

'It will stand up tomorrow,' said Christopher confidently. 'It's got to. It can't not!'

Mr Duffy, the caretaker, came in with his bucket and mop. 'Who put that frog in the basin?'

'I did,' said Weefy. 'He's got to be kept damp.'

'He's made everything damp,' said Mr Duffy. 'You go and take a butcher's. You left the tap on and the basin overflowed.'

He went clanking crossly away.

'What's a butcher's?' Sam asked Mrs Green as Weefy rushed out.

'A look,' she explained. 'Butcher's hook, look. It's rhyming slang.'

The Baby Class had taken Frog into

their classroom. Weefy went in. 'They can play with him, but they must pour water over him because he needs to be kept damp,' he told pretty Miss Binns. 'And also it makes his colours come up.'

'They'll do that,' pretty Miss Binns promised him. 'There's nothing they like doing better than pouring water over things.'

'*Now*,' said Mrs Green, when Weefy got back, 'let's get on. I want to tell you about the sun.' She picked up a yellow chalk and drew a golden whirl on the board. 'The sun is really a star.' Sam felt his mind go whirling off out of the classroom and into Magic Mountain where the Magician's daughter sat with her sad, frozen face. It seemed the most terrible thing to him to live in this astonishing world full of marvels and not to smile.

We'll make her smile, he thought fiercely, and speak, and laugh. We jolly well *will*!

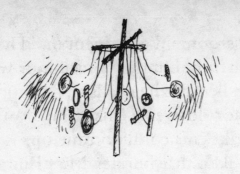

5 Will She Smile?

'*That*,' said Ivy, pointing. 'It's got to be
that.'

Top Class agreed. 'She'll have to smile at
that. It's so pretty!'

On the platform, on the faded flowers
and worn patterns of Mrs Green's magic
mat, stood all the things that Top Class
had made on Wednesday afternoons: Billy
Bottom's lopsided windmill, Weefy's
wind–sock, Russ's jumbo paper dart and
other triumphs. But best of all, best by far
of all, were the wind–chimes that Nargis

had made from milk bottle tops and from painted pasta that Italian Tina had given her.

Tina lifted the wind-chimes up now and blew on them. The milk bottle tops knocked against each other and made a tiny music.

'Take your bubble picture, too, Nargis,' commanded Ivy. 'In fact, let's take everything. She might like to play with them, don't you think, Scales?'

'No,' said Scales, who was lying on his back puffing at the paper spirals hanging above the radiator. His warm breath was making them twirl like waltzing snakes. 'She's a dreary girl. She doesn't play with anything.'

'She'll play with them, 'course she will,' chorused confident Top Class, gathering up the wind-toys and marching down to the green curtains and swishing them open. But – no magic! The wooden racks of boxes and bundles stayed solid and unmoving.

'Come back,' called Scales. 'This term is Flight! So – let's fly!'

'We can't *all* get on your back,' Ivy called back crossly, '*and* we're carrying things.'

'So ask Mrs Green if you can take the magic mat out on to the grass,' said Scales, rolling over.

Mrs Green was standing on a chair on a table wrestling with a huge picture that had to go up on the wall. Most of the picture was resting on her head and the rest hanging down over her shoulders.

'Mrs Green,' cried Top Class, 'Scales says can we take the magic mat out on the grass, please?'

'I don't believe Scales said any such thing,' said Mrs Green from under the picture, 'but yes, you can. The grass is still dry.'

She fired her staple-gun at the picture and got a bit of it flattened out against the wall. Top Class lifted the magic mat off the platform and carried it to the door, Scales walking beneath it, so as not to disturb Mrs Green.

They laid it on the grass behind the may tree and sat down carefully on it. Scales looked at Nargis who clapped her hands and cried, 'Take us to Magic Mountain! Oh, it's like the Arabian Nights!'

The mat lifted up, got hooked for a moment on a scratchy branch, freed itself and lifted higher still. Then it rippled forward, Top Class giggling with excitement and the wind-chimes tinkling like laughter.

'It's not very fast,' said Sebastian disparagingly. Immediately, the mat

stiffened and sliced through the air like a high-speed knife. The giggles changed to shrieks and the milk bottle tops streamed backwards and were silent.

'You stupid boy,' bellowed Ivy, thumping Sebastian, 'you've made it cross.'

'We'll fall,' shouted Dinny, clutching Sam.

'I'm going to be sick,' wailed Russ.

The mat slowed down and went steadily, but crossly, on (they could feel its crossness) until it landed on a flat-topped rock outside the Magician's cave. The minute the last child was off, it rolled itself up and lay there stiff as a stick.

'It's got the grumps,' said Weefy. 'Let's go in and see the Magician's daughter.'

But Sam put his hand out and stroked the mat on its canvas underside. 'Thank you for bringing us. Have a nice nap.'

The mat unrolled and draped itself over the rock.

They found the Magician blowing

down a long thin tube before a red-hot
furnace. At the other end of the tube, a
bubble grew and grew.

'He's glassblowing,' cried Ivy. 'I saw
that on the Isle of Wight.'

'We've brought the Gift of Air to break
the spell on your daughter,' Sam said in a
loud voice, 'and some wind-toys for her to
play with.'

The Magician stopped blowing, tapped

the glass bubble off the end of the tube and laid the tube aside. He looked at the wind-chimes and the wind-toys. He's not impressed, thought Sam watching him. He always glooms. 'Well,' sighed the Magician, 'well, let's see, shall we?'

He led them to the little cave. Top Class gasped. It was full of glass bubbles, different sizes, different colours, so lovely they made your lips smile, your hands reach out, but the Magician's daughter sat amongst them and her lips and hands never moved.

Nargis put her wind-chimes down. The Magician lifted his hand. The tiniest zephyr stirred the milk bottle tops. A delicate little tune came threading out. 'There,' said Top Class, 'isn't that pretty? It's for *you*.' But the little girl said not a word.

'Show her your bubble picture, Nargis,' ordered Ivy.

Nargis held it up. Hundreds of bubbles of different hues had burst against the paper leaving coloured circles. It made Top Class think of fields of summer flowers, clouds at sunset, but it did nothing for the Magician's daughter.

'Let's take her outside and show her our things there,' suggested Billy Bottom stoutly. He took the little girl's hand and led her out into the sunlight. 'You sit there and watch.' He put his lopsided windmill down and, such is the power of Magic Mountain, the crumpled sails began to turn, faster and faster. Top Class cheered, but the Magician's daughter just watched.

'I expect she'd like something clever,' remarked Christopher. 'After all, she *is* a magician's daughter.' He asked the Magician for two candles and one big jar and one small jar. Then he lit the candles and put the jars over them. 'Now you'll see that the candle under the small jar will go out first, because it hasn't got as much air as the candle under the big jar and it *must* have air to burn.' All watched and, lo, Christopher's words came true. The

Magician looked as if he *might* smile, if he could remember how, but his daughter just looked.

'We haven't succeeded *this* time, Sir,' said Sam, 'but we *will*.'

'Believe him, Mage,' urged Scales. 'Sam's my boy, I wouldn't pick a dud.'

'Thank you for trying, children,' sighed the Magician, 'but – it seems nothing made with fingers is going to break the witch's spell.'

Top Class picked up its wind-toys and climbed back on to the magic mat, and sat down tidily without squabbling. The sad shock of failure subdued them and though the journey back was swift and smooth, they could not enjoy it.

'Well!' cried Mrs Green when they carried the mat in. 'That airing's done it good. The nap looks like new!' She stroked the flowery pattern with pleasure, and it *did* look richer and thicker and brighter. Sam remembered his words to the mat, 'Have a good nap!' Tricky old

Magic Mountain! It *could* work magic, and he felt his heart grow buoyant as hope crept in.

'Sit on the mat, everyone, and I'll tell you the story of Daedalus and Icarus,' said Mrs Green and told them how Daedalus, the clever engineer, made himself a pair of wings from birds' feathers and stuck them on with wax, and made another pair for his son Icarus. It was a good story, but not a jolly one.

'Poor old Ic,' said Billy Bottom, 'to fly so high and then go smash into the sea.'

'He was over-confident,' said Mrs Green. 'A bad thing to be.'

As they put their chairs up to go home, Sam said, 'We shall have to try the other way.'

'What other way?' asked Weefy.

'Ask the King to change his mind.'

'Change his mind to what?'

Ah, indeed, to what?

6 Trouble On The Mountain

The next few days were rather gloomy.
The bright sparkly weather went and cold
grey weather came. Top Class felt dull.
They'd failed to make the Magician's
daughter smile, the balloon still hung over
the side of the milk bottle, and Science was
getting harder.

Mrs Green was teaching them about the
earth going round the sun. 'We'll do it in
the playground because we need space.' It
was very uncomfortable. The wind flung

grit and leaves, dust and sweet-papers in their faces. Mrs Green drew a small chalk circle on the ground. 'That's the sun. Ivy, you be the sun.' Ivy stepped importantly into the circle. Mrs Green drew a long flattened circle round her. 'The earth doesn't travel round the sun in a proper circle,' she explained. 'It goes in an ellipse, *and*,' she stood up, red-faced and panting, 'the sneaky old earth doesn't just go round the sun, it goes round spinning on its own axis – that is, spinning as it goes. Weefy, you be the earth.'

So Weefy stepped on the chalk line and began to spin round on his toes as he travelled along the ellipse.

'He'll get dizzy,' screamed Top Class – and Weefy did! He spun off course and banged into Billy Bottom.

'And that's not all,' said Mrs Green. 'Not content with doing two difficult things, travelling round the sun *and* spinning on its own axis, the sneaky old earth does it all on a slant!'

'I can't do a slant,' gasped Weefy. 'I'll fall over.'

'We'll go in,' said Mrs Green, 'and I'll show you on the globe. There's altogether too much air out here!'

In the classroom, she took the big globe, tilted it and walked round Ivy, spinning it as she went.

'Why doesn't all the water run off?' Russ asked. 'The rivers and seas and things?'

'Because they're glued on,' said someone.

'Because of gravity,' said Mrs Green.

She picked up a rubber, held it up, and dropped it. 'That's gravity. The pull of the earth. If you jump up, you come down.'

All through the morning the wind increased and things flying past the window increased! Sam saw a dustbin lid, a roof tile, a flappy bit of roofing felt and – *and* a little dragon with a furious, frightened face! The little dragon went scuttering along the glass, clung to the edge of the bricks, and vanished!

Sam poked Christopher. 'That was Scales' littlest cousin! She must be looking for him. Something must have happened.'

The sky darkened, the wind howled. Mrs Green switched the lights on, went out briefly, and came back.

'Miss Barley says indoor play. It's too dangerous to go out. Move away from the windows, children. This is a Fen Blow all right.'

A Fen Blow! Top Class quivered. Grown-ups always dreaded a Fen Blow, but the huge wind that sometimes tore across the flat fen fields, scooping up topsoil, lifting roofs and small dogs, was exciting. That is, if you were safe indoors!

At playtime, Top Class got out the games and puzzles, comics and cushions, while Mrs Green picked up her handbag. 'Be good. Jennie will be in shortly to sort out some stuff for me behind the green curtain.'

'She can't!' Top Class was indignant. 'Scales lives there!'

'Then he'll have to come out – or help!' retorted Mrs Green and went off to the staffroom.

Scales came out of the curtains, looking cross.

'Scales, your littlest cousin was trying to find you,' Sam told him.

Scales stopped looking cross and looked anxious.

'Trouble on the mountain and only

Grandrag there to look after my silly cousins. I must go. Thanks, Sam.'

'But we'll come too!' cried Sam, and he and Weefy, Tina, Billy and Ivy, Nargis and Christopher leapt up. The door opened and Scales shot under a table as Jennie walked in.

'Now, where's this stuff I've got to sort?' she said, swishing the curtains apart and looking up at the laden shelves.

Scales oozed out of the room behind her back and the children crept out after him. Together they sped down the corridor and out on to the steps.

'You *can't* fly in a Fen Blow!' shrieked Ivy, grabbing his tail. 'Don't be *silly*, Scales!'

'I've got to, but you and Billy will be too heavy. Go back and keep Jennie from noticing the others aren't there.'

He spread his wings and lifted up. Above the roof, the wind seized him and hurled him through the sky. Sam, Chris, Weef, Nargis and Tina clung on to all the bits of Scales they could, but the wind tore them off – and hurled them back, over and over again! The sky was so busy! It was full of traffic: bushes, garden sheds, clothes lines, scarecrows, and birds, poor birds—

'Those ducks are flying *backwards*!' screamed Weefy. 'Look at them, they're going backwards standing up!'

'They're being *blown*,' Christopher shouted in his ear. 'They can't control their flight. *Nothing* flies backwards, it's impossible!'

Scales struggled to fly higher. Beneath them rolled a vast black cloud, all the precious topsoil from the fen farms, all the precious seeds the farmers had sown.

Sam sneezed, Weefy sneezed, and then Tina, then Nargis. Soon they were all sneezing. Scales sneezed and *that* bounced them up and down! Then the huge wind gentled, the sky became blue, Sam wiped his eyes and saw that journeying with them were clouds and clouds of shining seeds, millions of seeds!

Scales cried out, 'Hang on, I'm going down.' He fell, rather than landed on Magic Mountain. The children rolled off him and lay breathless and bruised, looking up at the cloud of seeds which had stopped moving and was gently, gently floating down.

They sat up and began to pick and brush the seeds off themselves and every seed they loosened floated down and sank into the earth.

A squeaky piping began. 'Scales, Scales, Scales, oh dear Scales, you're here, and brave Sam and clever Nargis and Tina, and funny Weefy with his mouth open!'

All Scales' twenty little cousins began to run all over Scales and the children kissing them (hot little kisses) while Grandrag said in her crackly old voice, 'The King is coming with his army and a thousand bags of salt. You and I, grandson, must go down and fight him!'

Scales stared at her. 'Grandrag, we can't

fight the King and his whole army! We aren't big enough. There's not enough of us!'

'There's us,' squeaked his cousins.

'And us,' cried the children.

'Poltroon!' hissed Grandrag, her wings rattling with rage. 'You are a disgrace to dragons.'

The littlest dragon flew up and spat a red spark of anger in Scales' face.

'Scales is right,' said Christopher. 'The odds are against us.'

'We could go down and meet him,' Sam said slowly. 'Grandrag's right, we can't let him start killing everyone and putting salt everywhere. But Scales is right, too. If we go down to fight, the King'll just kill us.'

'We must plead with him,' said Nargis. 'Beg him to change his mind.'

'Make him ashamed of himself,' spat Tina fiercely.

'We're *children*,' said Christopher. 'Grown-ups don't listen to children. It doesn't matter how clever you are. The more you prove them wrong, the crosser they get.'

'I can argue,' said Weefy. 'I know how to argue. I've been on lots of demos with my mum.' This was true. As a baby, as a toddler, Weefy had gone on demos with banners tied to his pram or pushchair.

'But your mum did the arguing,' said Sam. 'Chris is right. The King won't listen to you. You're not a grown-up.'

'Then I'll disguise myself,' said Weefy.

Grandrag's old eyes gleamed. 'Fly to the cave, dragonlets, and fetch the brightest of my old skins and bring it back for our hero!' She turned a glowing smile on Weefy – glowing because a frail fire still burned at the back of her old throat.

The little dragons flew off and, presently, flew back holding a small, old, sloughed–off dragonskin. They put it on Weefy so that the head stuck up behind his head, the front legs and claws crossed over his chest and the rest hung down his back

and trailed on the ground. The scales had
soft, glinting colours and zigzagged in
strange patterns. The littlest dragon flew
to him, curled herself round his head and
lay still.

'There,' said Weefy, 'how do I look?'

The others considered him. As a rule, Weefy had a coming-apart look as though his clothes had been flung on him from a great distance, but now, robed in the dragonskin, crowned with a dragon, he had an all-of-a-piece air of power.

'You look – like a magician,' breathed Nargis.

Sam thought, Weef's always someone you look twice at, if only because you can't believe it the first time.

Grandrag snapped, 'Well? Do we wait here for the King to come and kill us or do we march?'

'We march,' said Sam. *Now!*

He swung round and set off with Christopher beside him, and the others fell in behind. Down and down they marched, down and down.

A noise came up to them: wagon wheels, whipcracks, and a voice issuing orders. 'The King!' whispered Nargis, clutching Tina's hand. 'The King,' said Christopher and his lip trembled.

'Look brave,' ordered Sam. 'Don't worry how you feel. *Look* brave!'

So they looked brave and marched on, their hearts in their mouths and, where their hearts should have been, small cold lumps of fear.

7 Weefy Gets The Wind Up

Even without knowing they were going to
meet an angry king, it was not easy going
down the mountain. The stony path was
slip-slidey, a cold wind bothered them and
there was a chill, purply-grey look to
everything.

'It's autumn on Magic Mountain, isn't
it?' Sam called back to Scales.

'Yes,' Scales answered, 'but it could still
be pretty if the sun would only come out.'

'The mountain is sad,' said Nargis.

'Or angry,' said Tina. 'Oh, look, look!'

They had come to where the mountain smoothed out into the foothills and they could see what they would much rather *not* see – the King with his soldiers and salt wagons!

The cold fear in every heart spread to arms and legs, fingers and toes, and every child found itself trembling violently. Scales leapt forward. 'I'll tear down like a Fen Blow and knock the King off his horse!'

'We will, too,' shrilled his cousins. 'We'll push all the knights off! *Splat!* they'll go!'

Grandrag creaked forward. 'I can still blow a few sparks. I'll stampede the horses.'

'Stop,' cried Sam. 'Stop! We must have a plan.'

'I've got a plan,' cried Nargis and went flitting among the rocks and heather and little stunted trees, stopping and stooping, pulling and plucking. Tina bounded forward to help her and, presently, both came back with their arms full of twigs and grasses, little shells and stones.

'Now,' ordered Nargis, 'everyone make a wind-chime. We've found stones and shells with holes in them and we can tie them on to the twigs with grass stems.'

At once fear left each heart (well, almost) and hope pushed in. In a magically short space of time, everyone, even Grandrag with her slow old claws, had made a wind-chime and Tina had decorated hers with red and blue berries.

'Now,' said Nargis again, 'we'll go in procession. Tina and I first, dancing and singing – that will surprise the King and he'll stop and stare. Then you, Sam, and Christopher marching together, then Weefy by himself. Grandrag behind Weefy to guard him, and Scales at the end to keep an eye on everyone. The little cousins can fit in amongst us! Hold up your wind-chimes!'

They held them up and the cold wind shook out an angry little tune from the

stones and shells. If the King listens to *that*, thought Sam, it ought to frighten him. But privately he felt that the King would not listen.

'Well done, Nargis, I'm impressed,' praised Christopher who did not impress easily. 'You're a general!'

'Wait,' growled Grandrag, 'my turn now. Words and music are all right, but for battle you need hot blood!'

She began to breathe faster and faster till her old sides were going in and out like bellows and puffs of comforting warm air came out of her throat, making their cheeks glow and the wind-chimes ring like bells.

'*Now,*' cried Nargis, and she and Tina went twirling and skipping down the smooth slope with the others following in procession.

So dancing and singing, laughing and leaping, they came to the place where the King was and so perfect was Nargis' generalship that the King *did* spin round and stare, the soldiers *did* stop humping sacks of salt, the knights *did* stop drawing their swords. In utter silence the grown-ups gaped and glared as the children came on till Nargis and Tina stopped before the King, Sam and Christopher saluted, the little dragons fluttered to the ground and all the wind–chimes stopped.

'Who, or what, are these?' barked the King.

'Children and – er, dragons,' said a knight swiftly.

'We can see *that*,' snapped the King. 'But what—'

'Sire, we come to plead for Magic Mountain,' said Nargis, sinking gracefully to her knees, 'to beg you to change your mind. Surely, surely so great a king cannot wish to harm and kill?'

'*Shouldn't*, even if he does wish,' said Tina, not sinking to her knees, but stamping her foot and tossing her ponytail. 'It's a wrong and wicked thing to do!'

'And counter to your best interests,

Your Majesty,' put in clever Chris. 'A bare mountain is totally unproductive and a gold one would mean a high invasion risk!'

The King's black brows, which had shot up in astonishment, came down in an angry scowl. Oh, golly, we've made him mad, thought Sam, now he'll kill us. But Scales saw the danger and bounded forward.

'Listen to them, King, they are special children, they are in *Top Class*!'

'We do *not* listen to *children*,' snapped the King, who *had* been listening to children, 'and young dragons who roar at us will feel our sword.'

Sam came forward quickly. 'Y-Y-Your M-Majesty, f-forgive us. W-We're not used to talking to kings. We've never even spoken to our own Queen, but we *are* special and we've brought a special kind of boy to argue with – I mean to—'

Sam's mind twisted in knots. I'm messing this up, he'll just get madder, he thought. But the King wasn't getting angrier, wasn't even looking at Sam. He was staring in astonishment at Weefy, who was wafting towards him with the dragon wings lifting and falling and the patterns and colours on the dragonskin moving as though alive. The wind-chimes in Weefy's hand sang a cold little song and on his head the littlest dragon was shining like solid gold and glaring at the King with eyes as red as rubies.

'I'm not going to argue,' began Weefy because that was how his mother always began her arguments, 'because I understand why you're angry. But the Magician hasn't turned the mountain into gold because he isn't interested in turning mountains into gold. He isn't even interested in turning stones into frogs! But he *is* interested in blowing glass bubbles and he's *brilliant* at blowing glass bubbles. You ought to *see* the glass bubbles he blows—'

'What is this twaddle?' roared the King. Then, 'You are an odd boy.'

'I am,' agreed Weefy, 'and *because* I'm odd I can do things even boys cannot. I can jump off the ground, like this, and NOT COME DOWN!'

There was a gasp. A knight leapt forward and swept his sword beneath Weefy's feet. There was a huge 'OH!' from everyone except Weefy, who shot up higher still.

'This will be a bit above your heads,' he sang out, 'but I'm going to do an ellipse!' And he went twirling above the circle of upturned faces, but not above *all* of them because, 'An ellipse is a squashed circle. It's how the earth goes round the sun, only the earth does it on a slant. I can't do a slant – oh, yes, I can, oh, super!'

'Come down, Odd,' bellowed the King. 'You make us dizzy. Can you turn the mountain into gold?'

'Anything,' sang Weefy, spinning off course and getting dizzy. 'A mountain of gold, riches for ever, every neighbour astonished!'

'When?'

Weefy came down to earth with a bump.

'When?' he repeated vaguely. 'When? Well – er,' he remembered what his mother always said, 'you must form a committee and decide on a date. That's when.'

'Send your heralds to cry it on the mountain, Your Majesty,' suggested Scales hurriedly, 'and I'll carry the message to Top Class.'

'So be it, dragon.' The King turned to the children, but Weefy was waving his arms and saying to Christopher, 'Did you see that? I defied gravity!'

'But we will not be defied,' interrupted the King, who had never heard of gravity. 'Woe betide you, Wizard, if you fail, for no matter how high you walk on air, my archers' arrows shall find you!'

He turned away. The knights and soldiers laughed. Weefy looked aghast.

'Give me the dragonskin, Wizard,'

hissed Grandrag, 'and, grandson, take Top Class back. The dragonlets and I are safe for a few weeks.'

The children climbed silently on to Scales' back and went battling and buffetting through the Fen Blow till they tumbled untidily into the classroom. Scales slid beneath the cushions and comics just as Mrs Green came in.

'My goodness, Weefy,' said she, 'you are in a mess!'

8 Sam Discovers Something

'Well,' said Mrs Green coming in next
day, bright-cheeked and blown about.
'Now we have another word, or rather
two words, to add to our Wind Chart.'
And she wrote FEN BLOW under
CATSPAW and HURRICANE and
WHIRLWIND and put up a photograph of
trees blown down and walls tumbling.
'Now get your Flight books out and write
what the Fen Blow did to *your* home.'

'Blew the garage roof off,' said several voices.

'Blew our willow tree down,' mourned Dinny, a great climber. 'It fell on our Bramley apple tree and split it down the middle.'

'Blew our Yorkshire terrier up in the air on the end of his lead like a balloon,' said Ivy Grubb.

'Blew my dad's greenhouse down!'

'Oh, Sam, your poor dad! His precious greenhouse. What did he do?'

'Blew his top!' said Sam and everybody laughed.

'Well, write your best,' urged Mrs Green, 'because this is history, *your* history, and one day your grandchildren will read it.'

Sam began to write about the Fen Blow, but then, quite without meaning to, found himself writing about Magic Mountain and Weefy defying gravity.

At playtime a furious Top Class, who had been bubbling with anger ever since

yesterday hometime, gathered round
Weefy and demanded an explanation of
why he had promised the King to turn the
mountain into gold.

'I felt so buoyant up in the air, I could
have promised anything to anybody,'
explained Weefy. 'It felt so easy.'

'Well, it isn't. If the Magician can't do it,
we definitely can't. It's impossible,'
shouted Top Class.

'We don't know that,' objected Weefy,
sounding like his mother. 'The mountain
might do it. It's a magic mountain.'

'If it could, it would've. It doesn't want
to be salted.' Sam gazed at Weefy in
despair. 'Weef, we'll have to go back when
the King decides the date. We can't let
Scales down, and the King's archers will
shoot you dead.'

'Only dead on Magic Mountain,' said
Weefy, pushing his hair up into spikes. 'I
don't suppose I'll be dead here.'

'I don't see why you shouldn't be,' said
Billy Bottom. 'You might be.'

'Scales will think of something,' said
Weefy, part of whose oddness was that he
never seemed to worry about the things
other people worried about. 'There's lots
of time. The King's committee will take
ages to decide on a date. Committees take
ages.'

The bell went. Top Class went in, still
debating. Sam wondered if Scales *had*
thought of anything. But how can I get
hold of him? Jennie was still sorting out
the shelves behind the green curtain. The
curtains were pulled back, against the door
at one end and against the window at the
other, and she and Mrs Green were always
coming and going there. It was, at present,
totally *un*dim and *un*mysterious.

'What a gloomy Top Class!' cried Mrs
Green when she saw them. 'Cheer up,
we're going to do a lovely thing. I've put
out a balloon and a label for each of you on
your tables. You're going to write a
message on the label asking whoever finds
your balloon to please send it back and,

when you've done that, we're going to let them go in the playground.'

Well, that was better! Top Class rushed to the balloons and began blowing them up. Blowing up was easy, tying them was not. Some of the balloons escaped and went spurting across the room making rude noises that delighted Billy Bottom.

'Stop!' laughed Mrs Green. 'We've only got to write the labels. Mr Duffy will blow up the balloons with helium gas. The Seniors have very kindly let us have some helium from their Physics lab. Helium is lighter than air, so the balloons will stay up longer.'

Much excited, Top Class wrote out the labels. 'Put your name on,' said Mrs Green, 'and the school address.' She wrote the address up on the board together with the message.

'I'm writing my message in French,' called Christopher, 'in case my balloon gets to France.'

Sam curved his left hand round his label,

so that no-one should see who he was writing to nor read his message.

Then they all went into the playground where Mr Duffy was standing by the helium canister and Mr Duffy pumped helium gas into each balloon and tied the knot expertly.

'Hold your balloons up, everybody,' cried Mrs Green. 'Now, all together – let go!'

Hurray! To whoops and cheers of joy, the balloons rose into the air higher and

higher and went sailing off, getting smaller and smaller until they disappeared.

'Go to Spalding, go to West Runton, go to my nan at Boston, go to France,' shouted the children, 'go to America, go to Disneyland!'

'Go, go, *go*!' shouted Sam, but he did not say where nor to whom!

Then, full of fresh air and hope, Top Class went skipping in so buoyantly they might have been walking on air.

'That's a happier class,' smiled Mrs Green. 'Now come on the platform for our story – oh, look at our poor balloon! Is it never going to stand up?' She felt the radiator. It was only faintly warm. The balloon, a purple one, still hung down over the side of the milk bottle.

'Science isn't working?' suggested Dinny.

'The balloon doesn't know what to do?' suggested Russ.

'No, it's us,' said Mrs Green, 'or rather, me. There's something I haven't thought of or don't know about. So, that means something I've still to discover and that's exciting! Now, I'm going to tell you a true story about a pair of clever brothers and then I'll tell you the old Greek legend of Pegasus, the flying horse.'

So she told them about the two Montgolfier brothers who, on a windy September day in France two hundred years ago, sent up the first balloon. 'But it wasn't exactly *manned* because it carried a sheep, a duck and a rooster!'

'Like a fairy story,' exclaimed Sam.

'Invention is like a fairy story, Sam, because it is powered by imagination and nobody believes in it – till it happens!'

She opened a book and showed them pictures of the Montgolfier brothers with their balloon at Versailles.

'Were the animals all right?' asked Top Class anxiously.

'I'm glad to say they were. The sheep was quite calm about the whole thing, but the duck and the rooster were rather shocked.'

'I'm going to be an inventor,' said Weefy dreamily.

'Me, too,' said Dinny, 'but I'll invent medicines.'

'I shall be a scientist,' said Christopher. 'Actually, I'm one now.'

Top Class divided immediately into inventors and scientists, but Sam thought suddenly, I shall be a writer, and felt a window open inside him.

'Well,' said Mrs Green, 'if you have imagination and faith and stamina, which means staying power, so that you never give up, even when everyone says it's impossible, some of you may well invent and discover and even,' she smiled at Sam, 'write.'

Then she told them the story of Pegasus, the winged horse, striking his hoof on Mount Helicon in Greece and causing a fountain to shoot up. When the bell went

Top Class streamed out, bubbling and sparkling.

Sam walked home through the lane with Christopher and Weefy. They were waving their arms and arguing, but Sam was silent, thinking. I'm going to be a writer! That's amazing because I'm slow and stupid and not good at spelling, but it's true!

'Look,' shouted Christopher, suddenly, 'one of the balloons has come back. It's yours, Sam, I can see the label.'

They ran forward. Sam stood on Chris's back and got the balloon out of the branches of the hedge tree where it was caught. There was a message on the back of the label in green, spiky writing.

9 Chilling The Blood

It took a long time to clear up after the Fen
Blow and even longer for Mrs Green and
Jennie to sort all the stuff from behind the
green curtain and put it back. When it was
all back, Sam saw that though the shelves
were tidier, they were just as full, and
behind the green curtain it was still dim
and mysterious and green.

'You didn't throw much away,' he said.

'No,' agreed Mrs Green. 'I can't throw
away. I hoard. All teachers hoard. You

never know when something won't come in useful.'

'Dragons hoard,' said Sam. 'Scales has a hoard of his own. His father started it for him.'

'Has he?' said Mrs Green vaguely. She was putting letters into envelopes. 'Well, I expect he'll find it will come in useful. Now,' she said looking up, 'who knows what the thirty-first of October is?'

'Hallowe'en!' cried Top Class. 'Ghosts!'

'Yes,' said Mrs Green, 'lovely, lovely ghosts! This is an invitation to your parents to bring you back *after* school *on* October the thirty-first *in* your dressing gown and pyjamas! You can bring a pillow and a soft toy, *but* – teddies must be tough-minded and dolls stout-hearted. We don't want any squealing or fainting because – we shall be telling ghost stories!'

'Who?' cried Top Class.

'Miss Barley, me, the Rector and Miss Binns, though the Baby Class won't be coming. They're too young for ghosts.'

The thought of coming to school in pyjamas in the dark sent shivers of delight down Top Class's spine and there was more.

'There will be two competitions,' Miss Barley told them in Assembly. 'A painting competition and a story competition with a prize for the best Hallowe'en picture and the best Hallowe'en story or poem in each year, *and* a quiz for your parents!'

When they got back to the classsroom, Mrs Green wrote three words up on the board. 'Phantom. Spectre. Wraith. They all mean *ghost*!' and she turned her stick of white chalk on its side and drew three wraith-like shapes going 'Whoo-oo-oo!'

The days went by. The last leaves fell from the trees. Dusk came earlier. All the school was painting pictures and writing stories. Christopher was writing pages; so was Ivy. Even Billy was telling Tina about a ghost his uncle had seen and Tina was scribing it for him. 'It stood on the sea and shouted, "*Ahoy there, shipmate!*" My uncle leaned over the side of his boat and it walked towards him, lifting its legs up to let the waves roll underneath.'

Sam sat trying to think, but his head was wood. Not the ghost of an idea would come. He slapped his forehead, but all he could think of was Weefy and the King's archers. In despair he got up, put his head between the green curtains and whispered, 'Scales, *Scales*!' Nothing happened. He made an excuse, slipped out of the classroom and stole into the empty television room and called Scales by his magic name that no-one else knew, '*Sep-dibby-di-dum.*' He waited, and waited. Surely, *surely* Scales must answer his secret name. '*Sep-dibby-di—*' Flump, thump, bump, Scales landed beside him with a groan, 'Ouch!'

'What's up, Sam?' panted Scales.

But, 'What's up with *you*?' asked Sam staring, for one of Scales' wings hung awkwardly, one hind leg looked hurt and the spike on the end of his tail was bent.

'You first,' said Scales briskly. 'I asked first, so you tell first.'

'I'm worried about Weefy and the King's archers. I'm *supposed* to be writing a ghost story, but I *can't* because I've got Weefy in my mind!'

Scales swelled importantly. 'Pitch him out then because *I* shall save Weefy. At the very moment when the archers are about to let fly, I shall come on and astonish them! They will be transfixed with astonishment.'

Sam looked doubtful. Privately he felt that Weefy might be transfixed first.

'You'll have to time it very fine,' he said anxiously.

'To the split second,' replied Scales grandly. 'There'll be Weefy, dancing about in the air waving his arms, *not* turning the mountain into gold, there'll be the King black with rage, there'll be the archers with their arrows sharp as knives—' Sam shuddered '—pointing at Weefy and *just* as the King roars "*Shoot!*" I appear and tragedy is changed to triumph. *My* triumph,' he added. 'Everybody looking at *me*!'

'But what *is* it you're going to do?'

Scales looked mysterious. 'The impossible! I'm practising now, that's why I'm so bruised.'

'It sounds dangerous.'

' 'Course it's dangerous, and difficult – it wouldn't be the impossible otherwise. Now listen, I won't have time to come and tell you when the King and the committee decide on the date, so I'll send someone. Now I must fly – or try to!'

With an effort Scales lifted off the carpet, a clumsy flap of his bad wing catching Sam in the eye. Sam put his fist to his eye, and when he took it away Scales had gone.

October the thirty-first came. The school was full of ghosts, in pictures, in stories, in poems. Bloodstained and blackened pictures (carefully bloodstained and blackened by Jennie) were blu-tacked about the hall and corridor with writing underneath: 'This ghost throws things about', 'This Irish ghost wails before a death', 'This unholy thing sucks blood from its sleeping victims'.

'That's the Parents' Quiz,' explained Christopher. 'They've got to write down what sort of ghost or monster it is. *That* one,' he said pointing, 'is a vampire.'

At three-fifteen the children went home, and at six-thirty they came back (not the Baby Class). Dracula opened the door to them in a top hat and black cloak with two dreadful fangs and a bloodstained chin.

'Come in, children, I'm thirsty.'

There was a terrified intake of breath, then Christopher said, 'It's Mr Duffy.' And – it was.

A lady all in white floated up the corridor carrying her head in her hand. 'Just going to get the milk for the cocoa,' she said to Mr Duffy.

'It's Jennie,' cried Dinny. 'I saw her eyes through that big stand-up collar.' In the hall Miss Barley in a black velvet cloak, holding a tall ebony cane and wearing a bonnet that would strike terror into a phantom, divided the children into groups and said, 'Ghosts and witches happen *inside* books. They are part of man's wonderful imagination. He made up ghosts and monsters to help him control his fears and make sense of a world he didn't understand. Enjoy them, and remember, they're only stories.'

Sam, Weefy, Christopher and Ivy found they were the only Top Class children in their group. 'Now, we're not going to scream,' said Christopher. 'Only babies scream.' Miss Barley led them to the television room. 'Put your pillows on the floor, children, make yourselves comfortable and I will tell you a story to make the hairs on your head rise up!' She sat down in a chair with the black folds of her cloak spreading about her. On the table stood a grinning turnip head with a candle inside it making a flickering orange glow. A wind moaned outside the dark window. 'Listen,' said Miss Barley in her soft voice. 'Listen!' Sam felt the back of his neck prickle, but (Top Class *don't* scream) he and Weefy and Ivy and Christopher sat like rocks and the hair on their heads did not stir.

'Well done,' said Miss Barley when she had finished. 'I see you have nerves of steel. Now, go on to the Rector who has promised to curdle your blood!'

'But we won't scream,' said Weefy, as they went. 'We'll keep our lips pressed together.' And they did not scream, though they felt their flesh goose-pimpling, and the other children screamed and clutched each other.

After the Rector they went on to pretty Miss Binns. 'That's not her!' gasped Ivy. 'It can't be.' But it was – with a wig of snakes and some of her teeth blacked out! Her story was frightful and many a teddy was glad to have his paw held and many a doll shut her eyes and cried, 'Mama, mama!' But the Top Class four, though they shuddered, did *not* scream.

'We're all right now,' they chortled as they made their way to Top Class for the last story. 'Mrs Green won't frighten us!'

But – nothing's sure on Hallowe'en. The magic mat was *not* on the platform, but down by the green curtain and seated on it in a chair was a silvery-green lady whose dress flowed over her like sea-water. Her face was whitey green, silver glitter sparkled on her cheeks and her eyelids were silver. A green scarf covered her head and at her feet was a shell as big as a melon and shaped like a melon.

The younger children whimpered and hung back. 'It's a sea-fairy.'

'No, it's not,' said Sam stoutly, 'it's Mrs Green. Come on.'

'Yes, come in,' said Mrs Green softly. 'You will be quite safe. This room has sheltered children for a hundred years. Put your pillows on the mat and cuddle down, and I will tell you of a ghost ship that sailed and sailed.'

She picked up the shell, pressed something and it lit up with a deep orange glow like a harvest moon. 'Listen,' she said. 'Listen.' And moving about, holding the shell lamp, her voice rising and falling like the sea itself, she began the story of the ghost ship. The children turned on their pillows and followed her with their eyes.

She's floating away, thought Sam, going into the distance. He felt the back of

his neck go cold and looked behind him.
Beside him, Weefy shivered and did the
same. Christopher and Ivy shuddered
suddenly and turned round. Up at the top
of the green curtains a broom handle
poked through. A wrinkly hand came out
and threw something at Weefy and a
witch's wicked face looked down at them
and grinned. Four screams burst out. The
witch vanished. Mrs Green came running
back.

'Who screamed?'

'Top Class,' cried the other children. 'Not us!'

'Top Class,' cried Mrs Green, laughing. 'Shame on you!' And she sat down amongst them and finished the story. 'Now, pick up your pillows and come into the hall for hot cocoa and biscuits!'

She led them out and Ivy went with her, but Sam and Christopher hung back with Weefy.

'What is it?' asked Christopher. 'Oh, it's one of the questions of the Parents' Quiz!'

'It's not,' said Sam. 'They're only in the corridor and the hall.'

Weefy unrolled the thick yellow parchment and they read:

To Wizard Odd
Be on Magic Mountain
In Five days time
To turn it into GOLD or PeRish!
By Order of the King's Royal Committee.

'Five days, that's next week!' gasped Sam.

'You've gone white, Weef,' remarked Christopher. 'White as a ghost.'

'In five days time,' said Weefy glumly, 'I'll probably *be* a ghost!'

10 Scales Does The Impossible

'So,' said Mrs Green next morning, 'did you all sleep well, or did ghosts haunt you? Weefy, you look a bit haunted? Did you have nightmares.'

'I have death thoughts,' said Weefy gloomily.

Sam put his hand up quickly. 'Mrs Green, five days from last night – will that be Monday?'

'It will indeed *and* it will be November the fifth which is—?'

'Bonfire Night!' chorused Top Class.

'And you're all looking forward to it!'

'Weefy isn't,' sniggered Sebastian.

'Weefy's mum doesn't approve,' said Mrs Green, 'and for good reasons. A lot of people and pets get hurt and, when the Guy is burnt, it reminds her that we used to burn *people* and that was horrible. But Bonfire Night properly managed is fun and leads us on to – Fire! What things do you have in your homes that use fire and could be dangerous?'

'Cookers,' said Top Class. 'Matches.'

'Dragons,' said Sam.

'Science, Sam, we're doing *science*.'

'That balloon isn't,' said Russ, pointing to the purple balloon still hanging over the side of the milk bottle.

'No, it's not,' sighed Mrs Green. 'That balloon probably does need magic.'

'Fire is magic,' mused Sam. 'It's beautiful and dangerous, it changes things and it can be good.'

'Fire properly handled *is* good. We cook

with it, heat our homes with it. Anyone know why blowing puts out a candle?'

'Spit,' said Russ.

'No, you blow away the oxygen. Fire needs oxygen, like us,' said clever Christopher.

Fire was more exciting than Air. You could see it. It was red. It was dangerous. It changed things. Top Class got hot discussing it.

'Instead of a Bonfire picture this term, we'll do a *Sun* picture. The sun is like a big bonfire, only burning gases instead of wood. It's a huge fiery star. Look, I've drawn a map of the solar system.' Mrs Green unrolled a long piece of paper with the sun and the planets marked on it. Christopher was deeply impressed. 'You've got all the distances right,' he said, amazed.

'Please, can I do the sun?' Weefy asked suddenly.

'Yes! You'll need a lot of gold paper, *all*

the red, orange and yellow tissue paper, and it'll mean a lot of cutting and sticking.'

Weefy was not good at cutting and sticking. He *was* good at drawing, particularly drawing the way things worked, but he wasn't good at cutting and sticking, so it was odd that he wanted to do the sun.

'Can we make a rocket to land on the sun at night when it's cool?' asked Russ.

'You can't land on the sun at *any* time, Russ, it would frizzle you up, but yes, you can make a rocket. That would be just right for Rocket Table! Get up on the platform and make it there.'

'We'll paint it red,' said Russ, clambering up on the platform with the rest of the Rocket group, 'because my red dart flew the furthest of all the things we tested in the playground.'

Sam offered to help Weefy with the sun, but Weefy refused. 'I have to do it myself,' he said and went at it with fury, getting gold and orange bits all over himself as well as the sun. So Sam painted Pluto, a pleasantly far-out planet.

While they worked, Mrs Green told them incredible things like the earth being ninety-three million miles from the sun and the temperature in the middle of the sun being probably fifteen million degrees centigrade. Top Class listened but couldn't take it in; the figures were too big to seem real. What *was* real was Weefy being shot with arrows on Monday.

'You could duck and weave,' Billy Bottom said to him, 'like my uncle who's a boxer.'

'Scales is going to appear at the last moment and astonish the King,' said Sam.

'*Whose* last moment?' enquired Sebastian.

'Then *he'll* get hit by arrows,' said Ivy. 'How stupid!'

By Monday, November the fifth, the Solar System picture was finished. Weefy's sun bulged out, deep deep red in the middle, glittering gold on the rim, with orange and yellow flames flaring from the edges.

'It's magnificent, Weefy,' praised Mrs Green. 'Now, go and wash your hands and splash your face. You look red hot!'

Sam slipped into the corridor with Weefy and together they went into the Baby Class cloakroom to wash. The bell rang and the classes went out to play. Weefy nipped into the Baby Class and came out with Frog making damp patches on his jumper.

'I feel braver with him,' he explained.

Together they walked down the empty corridor. There was a Class 3 picture of a witch on the wall. 'That's good,' remarked Weefy touching it, and shrieked as the witch's fingers snapped round his wrist like handcuffs. She sprang out of the picture on her broomstick and whisked him down the corridor and out on to the steps. Sam tore after them and flung himself on the bristly end just as she took

off with Weefy clutched to her front (and Frog clutched to Weefy's front). The twigs stuck in to him, his legs were frozen and the witch kept jiggling the broomstick to make him fall off, but he hung on.

After a time the broomstick zoomed downwards; Sam's head butted into the witch's bony back. Then the broomstick slowed, tipped up, and he rolled off on to Magic Mountain. Picking himself up he saw the witch shaking out her skirts and shoving Weefy towards the King who was standing amongst his archers with the Queen and Princess and courtiers on a platform behind him.

'Where's Top Class?' shouted the King, but the witch was tugging at a stick that was slotted down among the bristles.

'Just getting my wand, Your Majesty,' she wheezed. It came out and she made a noise like a cat spitting. 'It's broken!'

Sam felt his heart lurch and looked down at his hand. A broken bit of wand was clutched in his fingers. I've got half her wand! He whipped it under his jumper and crossed his arms over it.

'Half a wand and no Top Class!' exclaimed the King. 'Badly done, Witch. Now, Wizard, begin. Turn the mountain into gold.'

Sam put one hand under his jumper and squeezed the half-wand. Make Weefy go up, oh *please*, make him go up.

Weefy, looking astonished, and Frog, no longer stone but a real huge frog, went up, and Frog made an enormous hop down to the ground. Then a soldier shouted, 'Gold, gold, he's doing gold!' Weefy, some two metres above them, was plunging his hands into his pockets and flinging out glittering gold pieces.

There was clapping and laughter and shouts of joy. But, 'The mountain, Wizard, turn the *mountain* into gold,' barked the King and one of the soldiers screamed, 'It's paper, Sire, it's only paper!'

'Trickery,' roared the King. 'Archers, draw your bows. Shoo—'

Weefy began to duck and weave, Frog hopped up to Sam and croaked fiercely. Sam squeezed the half-wand and whispered, 'Frog them, *frog* them.' The soldiers dropped to their haunches and their bows clattered down. 'Bip-bip, bip-bip, bip-bip,' went the soldiers, looking bulgy-eyed. The Queen and the court hooted with mirth. The King shouted at the witch who raised her half–wand at the squatting soldiers and screeched, 'Be *men*!' Up, up, up they stretched, tall thin green *frogs* holding their bows in their webbed feet. The Princess laughed till she cried. Frog hopped up and down, croaking so

mirthfully that the witch pointed her half–
wand at him and cried, 'Be *stone*!' Frog
turned into a stone but went on being
mobile and rolled rapidly towards her. She
turned and fled, with Frog rolling after her.

The soldiers returned thankfully to
being soldiers. Weefy lay on the ground,
gurgling with laughter. The King strode
wrathfully on to the platform and the
Queen pulled him down beside her.

'Now,' cried Sam desperately before the King could recover, 'Your Majesty, Scales will do the IMPOSSIBLE!'

He flung up his arm to the sky and the half-wand fell out of his jumper and rolled on the ground. The day was dull and a grey mist covered the mountain.

'So,' snapped the King, 'where's this dragon then?'

Then – Scales *did* the impossible! There was a roar of disbelief, the King sprang up, the Queen, the Princess, the Court. Weefy leapt up, Sam stared. It can't be, it can't – but it was! Scales was flying—

'BACKWARDS!' shouted the King. 'By thunder, he's flying *back*wards!'

He flung himself back in his chair and shouted with laughter. Then everybody laughed. The Princess snorted herself into hiccups. The soldiers clung to each other, whooping till it hurt.

'Backwards! He's flying b–b– backwards!'

The sun came out, the sky turned blue,

the mist rolled away. Slowly, steadily, carefully, Scales flew backwards, drawing the mist with him. The mountain shone out, dazzling, brilliant, an unbelievable gold. Gold? *Gold*.

'It's gold!'

From peak to base – gold.

11 The Gift Of Air

Well, that was marvellous and magical and jubilant and victorious! Top Class never tired of hearing the story and Weefy and Sam never tired of telling it.

'But how did you get back?'

'I picked up the half-wand, didn't I,' said Weefy, 'and said, "I wish the others were *here*" and it whizzed us *back*!'

'I'd like to see Scales fly backwards,' said Christopher. 'I hope he comes soon and shows us.'

But Scales did not come, and in the end

Tina said, 'He is sulking. He did not like being laughed at.'

'No-one likes being laughed at,' said Billy, 'especially when they're doing something difficult.'

'Weefy must write him a letter saying he's sorry,' decided Tina. 'You can say you were laughing at the soldiers, Weefy.'

'I wasn't, but I will,' said Weefy.

So he wrote a letter on the computer and put, 'Sorry I laughed, it was the soldiers, you were brill.'

'You could say, "Laughter is a nervous reaction",' suggested Christopher. But Tina said no, that was making an excuse. 'Now we'll put it behind the green curtain because Mrs Green and Jennie have finished there.'

The next day the letter was gone and the day after another letter lay in its place. This one said in gold letters: VISIT THE MARVELLOUS GOLDEN MOUNTAIN. Underneath in Scales' spiky green writing was: *Make your arrival astonishing!*

'But how shall we go?'

It was plain Scales expected them to come on their own, but just going through the green curtain wouldn't astonish anyone, so what would?

'The rocket, of course!' yelled Russ and began clambering into it.

'But there won't be *room*,' panted Ivy, squeezing after him.

But there was, there was! That was the astonishing thing!

'It must be growing,' puffed Billy, shouldering in behind her, and it must have been, for there they all were, inside it!

'To Golden Mountain!' shouted Russ, pressing the button.

It was a wet, cold indoor playtime and gold must be better than dull, drear dankness. Only Tina and Sam felt sad. 'I don't want the mountain golden,' said Tina. 'It will be hard and ugly.'

'It will be slippery and glary,' said Sam. 'I don't see how anyone can climb it.'

But, 'Ten, nine, eight, seven, six, five, four, three, two, one, ZERO!' the rest of Top Class was shouting. 'We have LIFT-OFF!'

W–h–o–o–s–h, straight into the solar system! There was the sun, enormous; there was the moon, much smaller; there was the Earth, titchy; but they could make out the Wash and the Fens.

'But how do we get to the mountain?' wailed Sebastian, not a lad to be interested in space.

'It will pull us by its own gravity,' shouted Christopher. 'Everything's got its own gravity, even chairs and tables—' but no-one was listening.

'Something is pulling us,' said Russ. 'It's like being lassoed!'

Then, 'Look, look,' shouted Dinny, 'I can see gold.' The blackness of space vanished; there was a dazzle so bright they shut their eyes; a noise of cheering, and

Scales' voice saying triumphantly,

'Top Class, Your Majesty, *the*
astonishing Top Class!'

They had landed on a wooden platform,
a very big wooden platform Scales was
beaming at them, the King was greeting
them, the Queen, the Princess and many
glittering people were smiling at them;
Sam spotted the Magician, glittering like
the rest, the only one not smiling.

'Welcome, Top Class,' said the King.
'Behold our marvellous mountain!'

Top Class looked. It was true. Magic
Mountain was entirely gold; no other
colour could be seen. Tina burst into tears.
Then Sam noticed something. 'Tina, Tina,
it's—'

But the Princess was coming forward.
'Shut your eyes and hold out your hands,
Top Class!' Top Class obeyed. 'Open your
eyes,' called the Princess.

'Oh,' cried Tina, 'flowers!' For in their
hands were golden flowers. Real, but such
a bright, bright gold. And now they

noticed that everyone was wearing crowns and wreaths and buttonholes of golden flowers.

'It was the seeds!' cried Nargis suddenly. 'The seeds the Fen Blow blew here—'

'And the mountain magicked them,' laughed Tina. 'Oh, clever mountain!'

'As fast as they are picked,' the King said, 'they grow again. All our neighbours come to marvel and are astonished.'

'And bring us gifts,' murmured the Queen. 'The palace is stuffed with them. We are growing quite rich.'

The Magician came forward. 'The flowers are perennials. I have studied them. They will open each year on the same day and bloom for nine days.'

'So it wasn't Weefy who turned the mountain into gold, Your Majesty,' said sneaky Sebastian.

'It was the mountain,' snapped Tina, 'protecting its people. We ought to say thank you to it.'

'That is what we are assembled for,' the King told her, and he jutted his beard at the mountain and cried, 'To the mountain!'

And so, not with salt–wagons and soldiers, but with laughter and music, the procession moved off the platform and wound its way up the mountain, the golden flowers springing up again as they passed and gentle zephyrs cooling their faces.

At the dragons' cave, Scales' twenty
little cousins and Grandrag were
waiting. The procession stopped. The
mountain shook and a tongue of flame
came out of a crack above their heads and a
voice as deep as the mountain rumbled,
'Offer the Gift.'

The Magician came forward and put a
glass model of the mountain, so
marvellously blown you could see the
caves and passages with the dragons and
people inside them, on a ledge before the
crack.

'We offer the Gift,' the Magician said
humbly.
'Is it good?'

The rumbling voice said, 'Put your hand in, Glassblower, and pick up a red or a white pebble.'

The Magician stretched his arm into the crack up to the shoulder. Then – he pulled it out and held up a – white pebble.

'Good,' said Scales. 'Dad likes it. I thought he would. If he didn't, the pebble would have been red and Dad would have come roaring down and laid waste the King's land. He was FURIOUS when he got home and found what the King had planned to do.'

The procession wound back down the mountain more musically and merrily than before (Sam noticed that the King's musicians had wind-chimes, very elaborate ones).

'Stay for the feast, Top Class,' commanded the King, but Top Class shook its head. 'The bell will be going and Mrs Green will be back.'

'Ah, the dreaded Mrs Green,' chuckled the King, 'we must not incur her enmity! But return next year for the Offering of the Gift.'

'What happens to the Gift, Scales?' Sam asked.

'It goes into Dad's hoard and the Magician makes a copy for the King and the King pays him,' said Scales.

'LIFT OFF!' yelled Russ and they went whizzing back. They were still spilling out of the rocket when Mrs Green came in. 'Oh, Top Class, that isn't indoor play, it's much too rough!'

November turned into December. Science ceased and Christmas began. Top Class cut out gold stars that looked like gold flowers. The purple balloon still hung over the milk bottle, a scientific failure, but no-one noticed it now, there was too much to do.

Sam still thought about the Magician's daughter, though, and was sad. He made his star into a flower and thought, I'll go and see her. Mrs Green was rehearsing the shepherds and the angels, Jennie was helping the others to finish their calendars. Sam got up quietly and slipped behind the green curtain. '*Please*, Magic Mountain, I want to see her,' and he was running down the rocky passages to the Magician's cave, and there she was, watching her father work, her face as sad as his.

'This is for you,' panted Sam, giving her the golden flower. It looked like a star in her little hand. 'We've had such a laugh this morning. Billy got his head stuck in

the donkey's head, Weefy tried to pull it
off and he fell over, and Billy—' Sam
spluttered into laughter. A fierce little fist
punched him, 'Go on, go *on*.' He
swallowed his laughter and went on. 'So
Mrs Green went to help, but she caught
her foot in one of the shepherd's crooks
and – Oh! Oh! Oh! she – she—'

'Don't stop! Tell the story!'

Sam mopped his eyes. 'All right, stop
punching me. I'll try.' He drew a deep
breath and with a great effort told the story
to the end. Then he jumped and stared,
'Hey, you spoke! You laughed! You—'

'Of *course*,' said the Magician softly, tears running down his cheeks into his smile. 'A story! A Gift of Air, made with breath.'

'More,' begged the little girl, dancing round Sam. 'What happened next?'

'I – I – must go,' spluttered Sam, surprised and stammering, feeling himself full of lovely swirling emotions.

'Of course, you must,' said the Magician, 'but come again, Sam Storyteller, and take this. Now, run, run—'

Sam ran, light as air, up, up, up and through the green curtain.

'What's that you've got?' asked Christopher.

Sam looked down at his hands. 'A bottle. The Magician gave it to me.'

'It's *terrifically* thin glass. Try the balloon on it. Heat ought to get through *that* glass.'

So Sam took the purple balloon off the milk bottle and stretched its mouth over the top of the thin, *thin* green bottle and put it on the radiator. Then Mrs Green called out, 'Come on Joseph and First King,' and he and Chris went up to the platform.

After that came the Nativity Play, and after that the Christmas Party, and after that the clearing up.

'What a lot of Science we've done,' cried Mrs Green, taking down the Solar System picture. 'Be proud of yourselves, Top Class. Oh!'

She stopped and stared. All looked. All gasped. The purple balloon was standing straight up like a crocus about to open!

'Magic,' cried Top Class.

'Science,' insisted Christopher.

'I expect it's magic when we don't know and Science when we do,' said Mrs Green. 'But I'm glad the experiment's worked at last, so we can end on a triumph.'

Came the unbelievable last day.

'Goodbye, children, have a happy Christmas,' smiled an exhausted Mrs

Green. 'Good *gracious*, how did that come there!'

For, in the clean bare tidy classroom someone had stuck a piece of paper on the green curtain. Mrs Green went over to it and read:

'*Who* is TCD?'

'Scales,' cried Top Class. 'He's Top Class Dragon.'

'So Scales thinks he's coming into Spring-term, does he?'

But of course.

THE END

A DRAGON IN CLASS 4
June Counsel

'Don't worry, I'll look after you. I've always wanted a boy of my own,' cried the dragon.

One morning on the way to school, Sam rescues a young dragon trapped in the chains of a swing. Scales – as the dragon is called – decides to join Class 4 and he brings lots of fun to Sam and his friends.

Scales moves into a cave on the Measuring Table in the classroom, and helps Sam and his friends with their spelling and painting, and in fighting off the school bully. He is Sam's special friend – a little, bouncy friend who is always full of super ideas!

'Imagination and humour work attractively together in a lively fantasy' *Growing Point*

0 440 86267 1

A DRAGON IN SPRING-TERM
June Counsel

'Here we are,' cried Scales cheerfully. 'Spring on Magic Mountain!'

Sam and his friends in Class 4 have a very special friend – a young dragon called Scales. They are all looking forward to seeing him when they go back to school for the Spring term. But Miss Green, their teacher, has put his cave away in the stockroom and firmly tells them that this term they will be doing new things, starting with a computer . . .

However, all dragons wake up in the spring, and soon Scales is back with Sam and his friends, leading them all up to Magic Mountain for a series of wonderful adventures!

An amusing and lively fantasy for young readers.

0 440 86209 4

A DRAGON IN SUMMER
June Counsel

'Summer term, Sam,' Scales beamed, *'and I'm in it!'*

Sam bounces back to school for the Summer term, looking forward to seeing his special friend Scales again. But will Scales, a young dragon, *want* to be in the term when he hears that Sam's class are going to act out a pageant of St George and the Dragon — and the dragon gets killed?

Luckily Scales knows the story of St George too, although *his* story has a very different ending, and he is determined to share in the fun. Soon Scales is right in the middle of all the excitement, bringing his silly little cousins along to watch the pageant, and whisking Sam and his friends off to Wish Wood and an enchanted island for a series of super adventures!

'A delight of lords and ladies, dragons and castles, witches and magic . . . highly recommended'
Recent Children's Fiction

0 440 86294 9

A SELECTED LIST OF TITLES
AVAILABLE FROM YEARLING BOOKS

THE PRICES SHOWN BELOW WERE CORRECT AT THE TIME OF GOING TO PRESS. HOWEVER TRANSWORLD PUBLISHERS RESERVE THE RIGHT TO SHOW NEW RETAIL PRICES ON COVERS WHICH MAY DIFFER FROM THOSE PREVIOUSLY ADVERTISED IN THE TEXT OR ELSEWHERE.

☐	86370 4	**OPERATION GADGETMAN!**	*Malorie Blackman*	£2.99
☐	86294 9	**A DRAGON IN SUMMER**	*June Counsel*	£2.50
☐	86267 1	**A DRAGON IN CLASS 4**	*June Counsel*	£2.99
☐	86209 4	**A DRAGON IN SPRING-TERM**	*June Counsel*	£2.50
☐	86332 5	**TABBY'S C.A.T.**	*Stan Cullimore*	£2.99
☐	86297 3	**THE DEMON PIANO**	*Rachel Dixon*	£2.99
☐	86299 X	**THE WITCH'S RING**	*Rachel Dixon*	£2.99
☐	86314 7	**THE GENIE OF THE LAMPOST**	*Rachel Dixon*	£2.99
☐	86327 9	**THE THING IN BABLOCK DIP**	*Rachel Dixon*	£2.99
☐	86323 6	**EATING ICE CREAM WITH A WEREWOLF**	*Phyllis Green*	£2.99
☐	86277 9	**SHRUBBERY SKULDUGGERY**	*Rebecca Lisle*	£2.50
☐	86325 2	**THE WEATHERSTONE ELEVEN**	*Rebecca Lisle*	£2.99
☐	86337 6	**FINDERS KEEPERS**	*Rebecca Lisle*	£2.99
☐	86262 0	**ROBBIE AND THE GANGSTERS**	*Victoria Whitehead*	£2.99